DISNEP
MEET THE ROBINSONS
Me, Myself, and the Bowler Hat Guy

Adapted by Annie Auerbach
Illustrated by Ron Husband and The Disney Storybook Artists
Designed by Disney Publishing's Global Design Group

HarperEntertainment
An Imprint of HarperCollinsPublishers

D1517691

HarperCollins®, ✿®, and HarperEntertainment™ are trademarks of HarperCollins Publishers.

Meet the Robinsons: Me, Myself, and the Bowler Hat Guy
Copyright © 2007 Disney Enterprises, Inc.
RADIO FLYER is a registered trademark of Radio Flyer, Inc. and is used with permission.
Printed in the United States of America. All rights reserved. No part of this book may be used or reproduced in any manner whatsoever without written permission except in the case of brief quotations embodied in critical articles and reviews. Printed in the United States of America. For information address HarperCollins Children's Books, a division of HarperCollins Publishers, 1350 Avenue of the Americas, New York, NY 10019. www.harpercollinschildrens.com

Library of Congress catalog card number: 2006937679
ISBN-10: 0-06-112468-0 — ISBN-13: 978-0-06-112468-6

First Edition

I am the Bowler Hat Guy, an evil, wicked villain! Mwa-ha-ha! I have all the makings of a villain—a nasty laugh, a wiry moustache, and a cruel robotic sidekick named Doris, who's also my bowler hat!

Our villainous deeds include stealing inventions from small children.

I laugh wickedly when I do so. Mwa-ha-ha! Alas, Doris cannot join me in my wicked laughter because she only speaks in beeps.

Too bad.

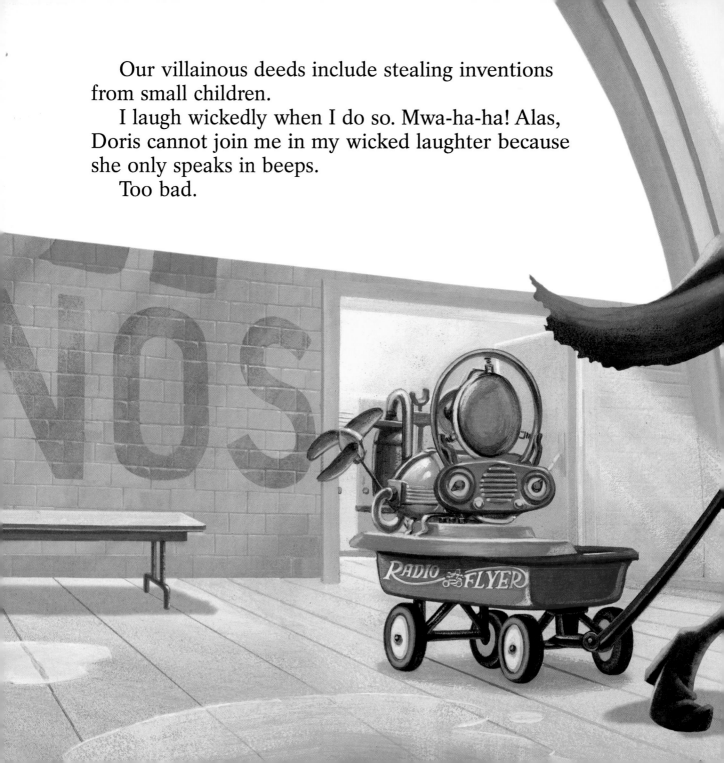

I bet you are wondering how I, the great and powerfully villainous Bowler Hat Guy, met my bowler hat?

Well, Doris and I met throwing toilet paper and eggs at the office of an invention company, Robinson Industries. She had just escaped from the building, after being rejected by that silly company.

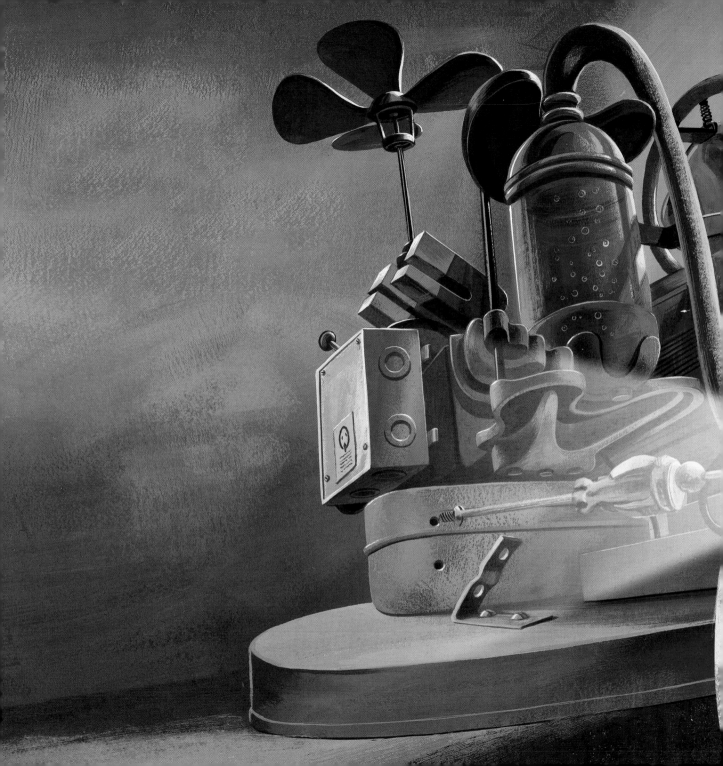

Yes, Doris is my partner, though all the truly wicked ideas are mine, mine, mine! (Well, okay, she's smarter than I am, but only because she's a robot.)

Sometimes when I steal things, I grab all the credit and even try to *take over the future*! Doris helps! That's why I keep her by my side—or at least close by. Too bad I don't always listen to her.

Once, Doris and I came deliciously close to changing the future forever. But, in the end, our plans were ruined and the future remained a sunny, cheery place. Drats!

On one of my more dastardly missions, I stole a
Time Machine! It was easy because that silly boy Wilbur
Robinson (whom I am *not* mentioning in this book)
left his garage door open.

So wonderfully simple and wicked at the same time! I do believe it was one of my cleverest evil tricks ever!

I traveled back in time to meet with myself as a child. I persuaded my younger self to hold all the sadness inside until it turned to bitterness!

"Everyone will tell you to move on, but don't!" I commanded in my most villainous voice. "Let it fester and boil inside of you!"

On another occasion, my attempt to capture an enemy with a frog didn't succeed. Luckily, I came up with a new brilliantly wicked idea—bring a T. rex from the past!

It was so evil! Of course, Doris was rather proud of me for being so smart.

One of Doris's mini bowler hats got destroyed, but we villains don't care much about our sidekicks, not to mention our sidekicks' sidekicks.

More importantly, the dinosaur had teeny tiny arms, so he just couldn't reach that blasted boy! Such a shame, since he had really big, sharp teeth!

You must be wondering (I know you are), what evil is Bowler Hat Guy up to now? Alas, I have changed. Some kid helped me catch a baseball. Long story. Too boring for a villain book.

To put it simply, I was angry and bitter, and now I'm—well—happy.

Doris went her own way, but that's fine. As you can see,
I am no longer a villain, and the future looks rather nice.
Turns out, enjoying life isn't so bad, after all.